LA MOMIA DE GUANAJUATO

Lah MO-mee-ah
deh Gwah-nah-HWAH-toh

★ Dug up from his tomb at Santa Paula cemetery, he has been chasing people since 1865. He hides out at the Guanajuato City Museum.

★ **Birth Name:** Dr. Remigio Leroy

★ **Lucha style:** Likes to bite

CABEZA OLMECA

Cab-EH-zah Ol-MEK-ah

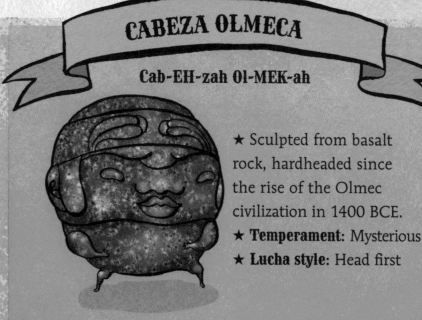

★ Sculpted from basalt rock, hardheaded since the rise of the Olmec civilization in 1400 BCE.

★ **Temperament:** Mysterious

★ **Lucha style:** Head first

LA LLORONA

Lah Jor-OH-nah

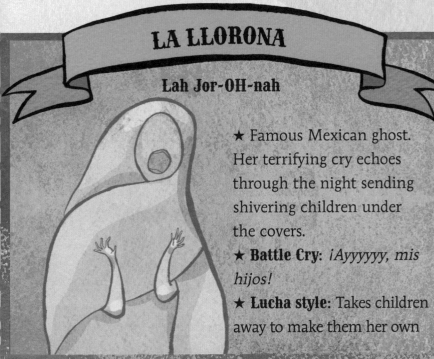

★ Famous Mexican ghost. Her terrifying cry echoes through the night sending shivering children under the covers.

★ **Battle Cry:** *¡Ayyyyyy, mis hijos!*

★ **Lucha style:** Takes children away to make them her own

EL EXTRATERRESTRE

El Extra-teh-RES-treh

★ Space explorer, first reported hovering over the earth in his flying saucer in 1947.

★ **Secret desire:** To see the world

★ **Lucha style:** Abduction

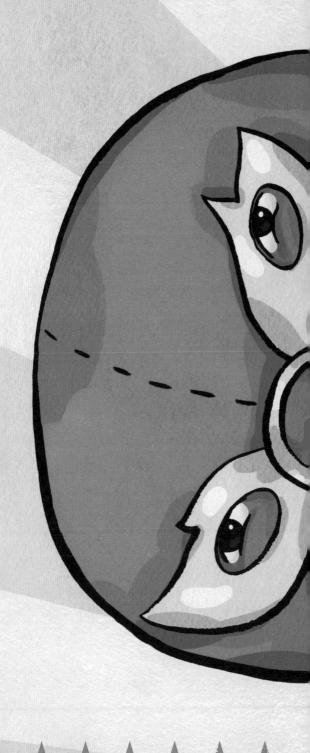

MAROMAS VOLADORAS

MASCARA VS CABELLERA

NIÑO
WRESTLES THE WORLD

YUYI MORALES

SQUARE
FISH

A NEAL PORTER BOOK
ROARING BROOK PRESS
NEW YORK

LUCHADORES

TÉCNICOS VS RUDOS

Niño!

SEÑORAS Y SEÑORES

Put your hands together for the fantastic, spectacular, one of a kind . . .

So superb are his talents that out-of-this-world contenders line up to challenge him.

Here comes the first one!

It is

THE
GUANAJUATO
MUMMY!

NIÑO
VS
LA MOMIA
DE GUANAJUATO

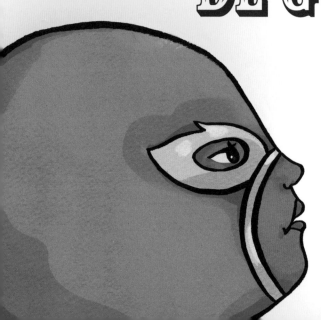

Oh, no!
What's a *niño* to do?

Niño defeats the Guanajuato Mummy
with the Tickle Tackle!

Uh-oh,

OLMEC HEAD awaits his chance
to bump skulls with Niño!

NIÑO
VS
CABEZA OLMECA

What will Niño do now?

Niño makes his Puzzle Muzzle move
and Olmec Head's mind is blown!
It is a real skull-cracker!

NIÑO VS LA LLORONA

Niño's Doll Decoy stuns the **WEEPING WOMAN** into submission!

NIÑO
VS
EL EXTRATERRESTRE

Marble Mash! Niño wins again!

There is no doubt,

no opponent is . . .

. . . too terrifying for him.

EL CHAMUCO

Niño does it once more.
Look at the Popsicle Slick!

Tick-tock!

Tick-tock!

Tick-tock!

But then the dreadful hour arrives. Oh, no!

His sisters' nap is over. Time for Niño to tangle with

LAS HERMANITAS!

Las Hermanitas are *rudas*.

Way to hold!

What a move!

If you can't defeat them . . .

join them!

LOS TRES HERMANOS

now
accepting

ALL COMERS

¡VIVAN LAS

Match dedicated to
KELLY "MARAVILLA" O'MEARA

ABOUT LUCHA LIBRE

Lucha libre is a theatrical, action-packed style of professional wrestling that's popular throughout Mexico and many other Spanish-speaking countries. In lucha libre, wrestlers, called luchadores, wear bright, colorful masks that represent everything from animals to mythical figures to ancient heroes and villains. They wrestle individually or as tag teams and often perform against the backdrop of stories with elaborate, twisting plot lines. Like Niño, many luchadores wear masks to hide their identities, some even outside of the ring. El Santo, the most famous luchador in history, was buried in his mask, and his true identity was never revealed to his fans. During matches, luchadores often attempt to unmask their opponents as a way of asserting dominance.

LUCHAS!

SQUARE
FISH

An Imprint of Macmillan
175 Fifth Avenue
New York, NY 10010
mackids.com

NIÑO WRESTLES THE WORLD. Copyright © 2013 by Yuyi Morales.
All rights reserved. Printed in China by RR Donnelley Asia Printing Solutions Ltd.,
Dongguan City, Guangdong Province.

Square Fish and the Square Fish logo are trademarks of Macmillan and
are used by Roaring Brook Press under license from Macmillan.

Square Fish books may be purchased for business or promotional use. For information on
bulk purchases, please contact the Macmillan Corporate and Premium Sales Department
at (800) 221-7945 x5442 or by e-mail at specialmarkets@macmillan.com.

Library of Congress Cataloging-in-Publication Data
Morales, Yuyi.
Niño wrestles the world / Yuyi Morales.
p.   cm.
"A Neal Porter Book."
Summary: Lucha Libre champion Niño has no trouble fending off monstrous
opponents, but when his little sisters awaken from their naps, he is in
for a no-holds-barred wrestling match that will truly test his skills.
ISBN 978-1-250-06270-3 (paperback)
[1. Wrestling—Fiction. 2. Monsters—Fiction. 3. Brothers and
sisters—Fiction. 4. Imagination—Fiction.] I. Title.
PZ7.M7881927Nin 2013   [E]—dc23   2012012989

Originally published in the United States by
Neal Porter Books/Roaring Brook Press
First Square Fish Edition: 2015
Square Fish logo designed by Filomena Tuosto

10 9 8 7 6 5 4

LEXILE: 260L

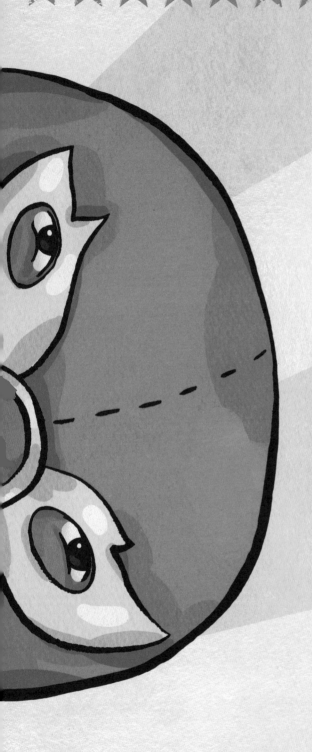

EL CHAMUCO

El Cha-MOO-koh

★ Powerful and rebellious, he likes to tempt people into doing bad deeds!

★ **Temperament:** Fiery

★ **Lucha style:** Placing obstacles and causing downfalls

LAS HERMANITAS

Las Er-mah-NEE-tahs

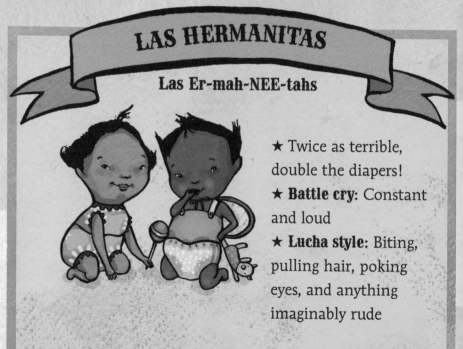

★ Twice as terrible, double the diapers!

★ **Battle cry:** Constant and loud

★ **Lucha style:** Biting, pulling hair, poking eyes, and anything imaginably rude

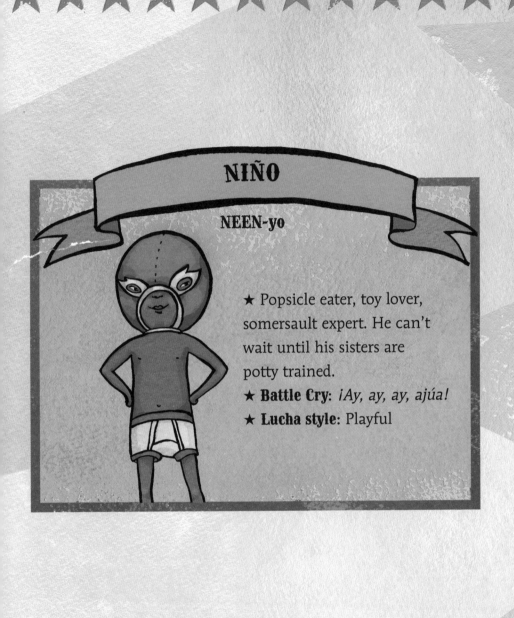

NIÑO

NEEN-yo

★ Popsicle eater, toy lover, somersault expert. He can't wait until his sisters are potty trained.

★ **Battle Cry:** *¡Ay, ay, ay, ajúa!*

★ **Lucha style:** Playful